STRANGER IN PARADISE

ROBERT B. PARKER

STRANGER IN PARADISE

Quercus

First published in Great Britain in 2008 by

Quercus
21 Bloomsbury Square
London
WC1A 2NS

A CIP catalogue record for this book is available
from the British Library

ISBN (HB) 978 1 84724 247 1
ISBN (TPB) 978 1 84724 248 8

10 9 8 7 6 5 4 3 2 1

Printed and bound in Great Britain by Clays Ltd, St Ives plc.

For Joan: *with whom I am no stranger*

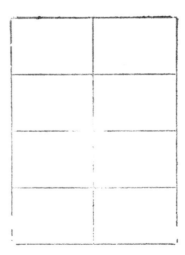

STRANGER
IN PARADISE

1.

Molly Crane stuck her head in the doorway to Jesse's office.

"Man here to see you," she said. "Says his name's Wilson Cromartie."

Jesse looked up. His eyes met Molly's. Neither of them said anything. Then Jesse stood. His gun was in its holster on the file cabinet behind him. He took the gun from the holster and sat back down and put the gun in the top right-hand drawer of his desk and left the drawer open.

"Show him in," Jesse said.

Molly went and in a moment returned with the man.

Jesse nodded his head.

"Crow," he said.

"Jesse Stone," Crow said.

Jesse pointed at a chair. Crow sat. He looked at the file cabinet.

"Empty holster," he said.

"Gun's in my desk drawer," Jesse said.

"And the drawer's open," Crow said.

"Uh-huh."

Crow smiled. He seemed entirely calm. But so much energy had been compressed into his physical self that he seemed ready to explode.

"No need," Crow said.

"Good to know," Jesse said.

"But you're not shutting the drawer," Crow said.

"No," Jesse said.

Crow smiled again. It was hard to say exactly what it was, Jesse thought, but there was a vague trace of American Indian in his features, and his speech. Maybe he really was Apache.

"Nothing wrong with cautious," Crow said.

"Last time I saw you was in a speedboat dashing off with a lot of money," Jesse said.

"Long time back," Crow said. "Longer than the statute of limitations."

"I'd have to check," Jesse said.

"I did," Crow said. "Ten years."

"Not for murder," Jesse said.

"You got no evidence I had anything to do with murder."

"Homicide during the commission of a felony," Jesse said.

"I doubt you could prove that," Crow said. "All you know is I

2

was with some people, and then I drove away in a speedboat to escape a shoot-out."

"With a guy who turned up dead, in a boat that turned up empty."

"Can't tell you about that," Crow said. "I got off the boat five miles up the coast."

"So you didn't come here to turn yourself in," Jesse said.

"I got some business in Paradise," Crow said. "I come here to see that you and I wouldn't be scraping up against each other while I was here."

"Two of my cops died when the bridge to Stiles Island got blown," Jesse said. "Some people on the island."

"Yeah," Crow said. "Macklin was a bad guy."

"And you?" Jesse said.

"Pussycat," Crow said.

"You gonna be in town long?" Jesse said.

"Awhile," Crow said.

"Why?" Jesse said.

"I'm looking for someone," Crow said.

"Why?"

"Guy hired me," Crow said.

"Why you?"

"I'm good at stuff like that," Crow said. "The guy trusts me."

He grinned at Jesse.

"And," he said, "I know the territory."

"Me, too," Jesse said.

"I know," Crow said. "And if we can't coexist it'll make my job a lot harder. That's why I stopped by."

"Who you looking for?" Jesse said.

"Don't have a name," Crow said.

"Ever seen him?"

Crow shook his head.

"Got a picture?"

"Not a good one," Crow said.

"Want to show it to me?" Jesse said.

"No."

"So how you going to find him?'

"I'll work something out," Crow said.

"What happens when you find him?"

"I report to my employer," Crow said.

Jesse nodded slowly. "As long as I have you in town," he said, "I'm going to do everything I can to put together a case against you."

"I figured that," Crow said. "I say you won't be able to."

"Limitation is sort of complicated," Jesse said. "There was bank robbery involved, kidnapping, these fall under federal statutes. I'll talk to an ADA tomorrow, see what they can tell me."

"Ten years covers most things," Crow said.

"We're going to watch you all the time you're in town," Jesse said.

"But you're not going to harass me."

"If we can put a case together on you, we'll arrest you," Jesse said.

"Until then?" Crow said.

"We'll wait and watch," Jesse said.

Crow nodded. The two men sat silently until Crow spoke.

"You know about me," he said.

"I checked you out," Jesse said. "When you were here before."

"What they tell you," Crow said.

"Be very careful," Jesse said.

Crow smiled.

"Macklin was good," Crow said.

Jesse nodded.

"I wasn't sure anybody could take him," Crow said.

"Except you?" Jesse said.

"Except me."

"Now you know," Jesse said.

Crow nodded. They were quiet again. Both men motionless, looking at each other.

"You let the hostages go," Jesse said.

Crow nodded.

"They were all women," he said.

"Yes," Jesse said.

They looked at each other some more. The room felt charged, Jesse thought, as if a thunderstorm were near. Then Crow rose gracefully to his feet.

"I guess we know where we stand," Crow said.

"Stop by anytime," Jesse said.

Crow smiled and went out the door, past Suitcase Simpson, who was leaning on the wall just to the right of Jesse's door, and past Molly Crane, who was on the other side.

Crow nodded at them both.

"Officers," he said.

And went on out of the station.

2.

Molly and Suit came into the office.

"I remember him," Simpson said.

"I called Suit in from patrol," Molly said. "I thought extra backup would be good."

"What'd he want?" Suit said.

Jesse told them.

"Brazen bastard," Simpson said.

Molly and Jesse both looked at him.

"Brazen?" Molly said.

Suit grinned.

"I been taking some night courses," he said.

"You have no idea who he's looking for?" Molly said to Jesse.

Jesse shook his head. "I'm not sure Crow does, either," he said.

"He say what he'd do when he found him?" Molly said.

"Said he'd check with his employer."

"Guy like that looking for somebody," Simpson said, "not good for the somebody."

"No, it's not," Jesse said.

"Think he'll find him?" Molly said.

"Yes."

"Hard to make a ten-year-old case," Molly said.

Jesse nodded.

"Isn't he some kind of Indian?" Simpson said.

"Claims he's Apache," Jesse said.

"You believe him?"

"He's something," Jesse said.

"He's a hunk," Molly said.

"A hunk?" Simpson said.

"He's absolutely gorgeous," Molly said.

"Isn't he a contract killer, Jesse?" Simpson said.

"That's what they tell me," Jesse said. "Probably part of his charm."

"Probably is," Molly said. "It makes him sort of exciting."

"Not if the contract's on you," Jesse said.

"No, but there's something about how complete he is, how, what, interior, independent."

"Power," Jesse said.

"Yes," Molly said. "He reeks of power."

"I guess I better take more night courses," Simpson said. "I don't know what you people are talking about."

7

"He's a little like you, Jesse," Molly said.

"Except that I just reek."

"No. You have that same silent center. Nothing will make you turn aside. Nothing will make you back up. It's...what do the shrinks call it...?"

"Autonomy," Jesse said.

"Yes. Both of you are, like, autonomous," Molly said. "Except maybe you have scruples."

"Maybe he does, too," Jesse said.

"For fantasy purposes," Molly said, "I hope not."

"Fantasy?" Simpson said. "Molly, how long you been married?"

"Fifteen years."

"And you got how many kids?"

"Four."

"And you are going to have sex fantasies about some Apache hit man?"

Molly smiled at Simpson.

"You better believe it," Molly said.

3.

"I wish to have nothing to do with this," Mrs. Snowdon said when Molly showed her a picture of Crow.

"Have you ever seen him before?" Molly said.

"No."

They were in the vast Snowdon living room in the huge Snowdon house on Stiles Island. Mrs. Snowdon sat on her couch with her feet on the floor and her knees pressed together and her hands clasped tightly in her lap. Suit stood across the room by the French doors to the patio. Molly sat on a hassock across from Mrs. Snowdon.

She looks too small for the gun belt, Suit thought. *But she's not.*

"Was he here with other men when they looted the island,"

Molly said, "and locked you and your husband up in the lavatory?"

"Late husband," Mrs. Snowdon said.

Her blue steel hair was rigidly waved. She wore a black-and-red flowered dress and a red scarf, and a very large diamond-crusted wedding ring.

"Was this man in the picture one of the men?" Molly said.

"I don't wish to discuss it," Mrs. Snowdon said.

"Are you afraid?"

"My husband is deceased," Ms. Snowdon said. "I am a woman alone."

"The best way to ensure your safety is to give us reason to arrest him."

"I will not even consider it," Mrs. Snowdon said. "It was a moment in my life I decline to relive."

"Has he threatened you?"

"Threatened? He's here? In Paradise?"

"Yes."

"My God, why don't you arrest him?"

Standing by the door, Suitcase smiled without comment.

"If you'd help us," Molly said.

"I'm not a policeman," she said. "It's your job to arrest him."

"Yes, ma'am," Molly said. "But we're not allowed to arrest anybody we feel like. At the moment our only hope would be that he could be charged with participating in a capital crime. Otherwise the statute of limitations applies."

"He has to have killed someone?"

"Someone had to die in a criminal enterprise of which he was a member," Molly said.

"Oh, God," Mrs. Snowdon said. "Gobbledygook. A number of people were killed, weren't they?"

"We have to be able to demonstrate this man's involvement," Molly said.

"Well, I'm not going to do your job for you," Mrs. Snowdon said. "What kind of job is this for a young woman? Why aren't you making a home for a husband and children?"

"I do that, too," Molly said.

She and Mrs. Snowdon stared at each other silently. Molly looked at Suit. Suit shrugged.

"I don't think you need to worry about him," Molly said. "He doesn't appear to have any interest in anyone from his last visit."

Mrs. Snowdon sat rigidly and said nothing. Molly let out some breath and stood.

"Thanks for your time," she said. "We can find our way out."

Mrs. Snowdon didn't speak, and they left her there, sitting in her iron silence.

4.

Jesse took Marcy Campbell to supper at the Gray Gull. It was June. They sat outside on the deck next to the harbor. It was still light and there was still activity in the harbor.

"Things not working well with your ex-wife?" Marcy said.

Marcy had platinum hair and wore skillful makeup. She was older than Jesse but still good-looking, and clearly sexual. Jesse knew that from experience. But he had also known it before he had the experience. Jesse always wondered how he could tell. He never did quite know, only that there were women who were insistently aware of their bodies, and of their sex. And somehow by posture or magic they communicated that awareness as insistently as they felt it. Marcy was the gold standard for such women.

"You think I only show up when there's a problem with Jenn?"

"Yes," Marcy said, and grinned at him. "Fortunately for me, it happens enough so that I see you a lot."

"Course of true love," Jesse said, "never did run smooth."

"You and me? Or you and Jenn?"

"True love? Both."

"Wouldn't it be pretty to think so?" Marcy said.

"I love you, Marce, you know that."

"Like a sister," Marcy said.

"Not quite like a sister," Jesse said.

"No," Marcy said, "you're right. Not like a sister."

The waitress brought Marcy some white wine and Jesse an iced tea. Marcy looked at the tea.

"Off the booze again?"

"Got no plan," Jesse said. "Tonight I thought iced tea would be nice."

"Got any other plans for the night?" Marcy said.

"Let's see what develops," Jesse said.

"Let's."

They read their menus, Marcy got a second wine, Jesse got a second iced tea. The waitress took their food order and headed for the kitchen. The shipyard next to the Gray Gull was silent now, and in the harbor the last of the evening boats were coming back through the gathering evening.

"Of course you remember the events on Stiles Island ten years ago," Jesse said.

Marcy seemed to immobilize for a moment like a freeze-frame in a movie.

Then she said, "When I was tied up and gagged and threatened with death by a bunch of cutthroats? Those events?"

"You do remember," Jesse said.

Marcy nodded.

"I wish I didn't," she said. "Forced to think about it, I also remember that you came and saved me."

Jesse nodded. The waitress returned with their salads. They didn't speak while she set them down and left.

"You remember one of them? An Indian? A man named Crow?" Jesse said.

Marcy again had a freeze-frame moment. It lasted longer than the first one had.

"My protector," she said.

"He's passed the statute of limitations," Jesse said. "But if I can get a witness or two to say he was involved in a felony that resulted in homicide, even if he didn't do the killing, I can get around the statute."

She shook her head.

"You won't be a witness?"

"No."

"Your protector?"

"Yes," Marcy said. "Stockholm syndrome, gratitude, call it what you will. I was lying on my back with my hands and feet tied and my mouth taped. There were five bad men in the room involved in a crime that would send them all to jail forever if they got caught."

Jesse nodded. "So they had nothing much to lose," he said.

"Nothing," Marcy said. "I was helpless, and they were free to do anything they wanted to with me. I couldn't resist. I couldn't even speak. About all I could do was wiggle. Can you even imagine what that is like?"

"No," Jesse said.

"That's right," Marcy said. "You can't. I wish I couldn't. I wish I could forget it."

"But they didn't touch you," Jesse said.

"No, because they knew that they'd have to deal with Crow, and they were afraid of him. Even Harry Smith."

"Macklin," Jesse said.

"I know. He was Harry Smith to me."

"If he'd needed to," Jesse said, "Crow would have swatted you like a fly."

"No," Marcy said. "I can't bear to think about it if I don't think of him protecting me."

Jesse started to speak and stopped. He put his hand out and patted her hand.

"Okay," Jesse said. "You came out of it okay, and that was because of Crow."

"And you."

"Me later, maybe," Jesse said.

They ate their salads quietly. The waitress cleared their plates and brought the entrées. Marcy sat looking across the table at Jesse. She was tapping her fingertips together near her chin.

"He came to see me," Marcy said. "Two days ago."

Jesse nodded.

"He threaten you?"

"No," Marcy said. "He was pleasant. Asked if I was okay.

Said he had some business in town, and thought he'd check on me."

"You believe that?"

"I believe what I need to believe," Marcy said. "If I stop thinking of him the way I do, I can't stand to live with the memory. I can't be Marcy. Can you understand that?"

"Yes," Jesse said. "I can."

5.

Molly sat with Jesse in his office.

"Nobody on Stiles Island will say anything about Mr. Cromartie," she said.

"Neither will Marcy Campbell," Jesse said.

"Even though you questioned her all night?" Molly said.

Jesse raised his eyebrows at her.

"I'm a law officer," Molly said. "I have my sources."

Jesse nodded.

"She feels he saved her life," Jesse said.

"All the hostages do," Molly said.

"All women," Jesse said.

"I told you he's a hunk," Molly said.

"Maybe they're right," Jesse said.

"That he did save their lives?"

"Yeah."

"Maybe they are," Molly said. "Still, a lot of people got killed, including two of us."

"And the only thing I saw him do was rescue the women," Jesse said.

"The other people," Molly said, "people in the bank, homeowners, other businesspeople, they won't even say he was there. They're scared, afraid to re-involve with him."

"Don't blame them," Jesse said.

"So, we got no case."

"No," Jesse said. "I talked to Healy. No warrants out on him. I talked to my guy Travis, in Tucson. Nothing. Crow doesn't seem to have been detected in a criminal act since he left here."

"With enough money to retire," Molly said.

"So how come all of a sudden he's out of retirement?" Jesse said.

"Well, he isn't, actually," Molly said. "He hasn't done anything but come here and say hello."

"So far," Jesse said.

Suitcase Simpson knocked on the doorframe and came into the office carrying a large foam cup of coffee.

"How's the crime situation at Dunkin' Donuts?" Jesse said.

"Under continuous surveillance," Suit said. "I got a little news."

Jesse waited.

"Wilson Cromartie just rented a place on Strawberry Cove," he said. "You know who the broker was?"

"Marcy Campbell," Jesse said.

Suit looked disappointed.

"You knew that?" he said.

"No, but what other broker would he know in town?"

Molly smiled at Jesse.

"She mention that to you last night, Jesse?" she said.

"No."

"Odd," Molly said.

Jesse nodded.

"You saw Marcy last night?" Suit said.

"She won't testify against Crow," Jesse said.

"Despite intensive interrogation," Molly said.

"Intensive," Jesse said.

Suit looked at both of them and decided to let it be.

"So I figure he's planning on staying awhile."

"Give us more time to bust him," Jesse said.

"If we can," Molly said.

"Sooner or later," Jesse said.

sipped again. If he didn't drink he might be with Jenn. If Jenn didn't try to fuck her way to fulfillment. If he were smarter he'd have let Jenn go and taken up with Sunny Randall. If Sunny wasn't preoccupied with her ex-husband. If . . .

Jesse walked to the French doors that looked out over his little balcony to the harbor. He had no illusions about Crow. Whatever his reasons for letting the women go ten years ago, whatever his reasons for protecting Marcy, if he really had, Jesse knew that had he needed to, Crow would have killed them all.

Jesse's drink was gone. He walked back to the bar and filled his glass with ice. He poured the caramel-colored whiskey over the ice and added the soda. He stirred it, and walked back to the French doors.

But Molly was sort of right. Jesse didn't know if he and Crow were alike. But there was something about Crow that clicked in Jesse. Crow was so entirely Crow. He belonged so totally to who and what he was. Crow probably enjoyed a drink. Probably had no problem stopping after one or two. Probably didn't get mad. Probably didn't hate. Probably didn't fear. Jesse took another drink and stared at the darkening harbor. . . . Probably didn't love, either.

"He's not missing much," Jesse said to no one.

Even saying it, Jesse knew it wasn't quite true. If he didn't love Jenn, would he be happier? He wouldn't be as unhappy. But was that the same? What would replace the sense of momentous adventure that he felt when he thought of her, which was nearly always?

Jesse made another drink. The evening had settled and the

21

harbor was dark. There was little to look at through the French doors. After he made his drink, Jesse stayed at the bar.

In a sense, loving Jenn wasn't even about Jenn. It was about who he was by being in love with her. So why not just let her do whatever she wanted to and love her anyway. What did he care how many men she banged? *Let her go about her business and I go about mine and what difference does it make?* He heard a low animal sound in the room. It was, he realized, him, and it had come without volition. He looked at his picture of Ozzie and shrugged. *Okay, so it makes a difference.* Was it more about him than about her? Did he hang in there because he would miss the high drama? He knew he loved her. He knew she loved him. He knew they couldn't find a way to make it work.

"Yet," he said, and drank some more.

7.

Crow was at a corner table in Daisy's, having an egg-white omelet with some fruit salsa, when Jesse came in and sat down at the table with him.

"Care to join me?" Crow said.

"Thanks," Jesse said.

Daisy brought him coffee.

"You want some breakfast?" she said.

Jesse shook his head. Daisy left the pot and swaggered away. Crow watched her.

"Daisy Dyke," he said.

"That's what she calls herself," Jesse said.

"Wonder why?" Crow said.

Jesse smiled.

"She was going to call the restaurant Daisy Dyke's," Jesse said, "but the selectmen wouldn't let her."

"Nice she's out of the closet," Crow said.

Jesse nodded and drank some coffee.

"Can't seem to put together a case against you," Jesse said.

"Can't lick 'em, join 'em?" Crow said.

Jesse shrugged.

"Doesn't mean I won't put one together," Jesse said.

"You do," Crow said, "I'm sure you'll tell me."

"First step is to find out what you're doing here," Jesse said.

Crow nodded.

"Be how I'd go at it," Crow said.

"You could tell me," Jesse said. "Save us a lot of time."

Crow shook his head.

"We're going to stay on you," Jesse said.

"How many people you got?" Crow said.

"Twelve," Jesse said. "Plus Molly, who runs the desk, and me."

"Four to a shift," Crow said, and smiled.

"We can be annoying," Jesse said.

"I know that," Crow said. "You were last time I visited."

"You're staying awhile," Jesse said.

"Maybe."

Jesse poured himself more coffee. The two men looked at each other.

"You know," Crow said, "and I know, that you aren't going to scare me off."

Jesse nodded.

6.

Jesse poured himself his first drink of the evening. The scotch whiskey looked silky as it slid over the ice. He added soda, waited for the bubbles to subside, then stirred the ice around with a fingertip. Jenn always used to say he should use a spoon, but he liked to stir it the way he did. He took a drink, felt it ease into him. He looked at his picture of Ozzie Smith on the wall over the bar. He wondered if Ozzie drank. Probably not, probably hard to do that backflip if you were a boozer. He raised his glass at the picture.

"I made the show, I'd be doing backflips, too," he said aloud.

His voice sounded odd, as it always did, in the empty room. If he hadn't hurt his shoulder he might have made the show. He

"I didn't figure I would," Jesse said. "But it was worth a try."

"I don't think that's why you came to see me," Crow said.

"Why did I?" Jesse said.

"You're just trying to get little sense of what I'm like."

"That why you came to see me, before?" Jesse said.

"Yeah."

Jesse drank some coffee. Crow finished his omelet and carefully wiped his mouth with his napkin.

"So?" Jesse said after a time.

"So you know I'm not going away," Crow said. "And I know you're not going away."

The tablecloth in front of Crow, Jesse noticed, was immaculate. No spills. No crumbs. It was as if no one had eaten there.

"Yeah," Jesse said. "That's about right."

8.

He was a smallish man with gray curly hair, pink skin, and a bow tie.

"My name is Walter Carr," he said. "I am a professor of urban studies at Taft University."

Jesse nodded.

"This is Miriam Fiedler," Carr said, "the executive director of the Westin Charitable Trust."

Jesse said, "How do you do."

Miriam Fiedler nodded. She was tall and lean and had horsey-looking teeth.

"And perhaps you know this gentleman," Carr said. "Austin Blake?"

"We've not met," Jesse said.

"I'm an attorney," Blake said. "I'm along as a sort of informal consultant."

"This is Molly Crane," Jesse said, nodding at Molly, who sat in a straight chair to the right of his desk. Molly had a notebook in her lap.

"We are here representing a group of neighbors," Carr said, "in order to call your attention to a problem."

Jesse nodded.

"You *are* interested, Mr. Stone," Miriam said, "I assume."

"Yes, ma'am."

"As you may know," Walter Carr said, "there is a plan being implemented to transform the former Crowne estate on Paradise Neck into an alternative school for disadvantaged students."

"Mostly Latino," Jesse said. "From Marshport."

"Paradise Neck is very elite. The streets are very narrow. The ocean impinges on either side."

Jesse nodded.

"There is no opportunity for expansion of the present road-ways," Carr said.

"True," Jesse said.

Blake the lawyer had a deep tan and snow-white hair worn longish and combed straight back. He was sitting quietly with his legs crossed, observing. It was an approach Jesse admired. Ms. Fiedler was impatient.

"For God's sake, Walter, the point is simple. The neighborhood cannot support busloads of unruly children coming and going in so narrow a compass."

"How about ruly children?" Jesse said.

Blake smiled faintly.

"Excuse me?" Ms. Fiedler said.

"Is it the number of buses?" Jesse said. "Or who's in them."

"Those buses will represent a huge traffic problem," Ms. Fiedler said.

She looked at Molly, who was writing in her notebook.

"What is she doing?" Ms. Fiedler said.

"Her name is Officer Crane," Jesse said.

"Whatever it is, what is she doing."

Jesse smiled.

"I don't know," Jesse said. "Molly, what are you doing?"

"I'm a female," she said. "I have a compulsion to sit near the boss and take notes."

"Notes?" Ms. Fiedler said. "This is an informal discussion. There's nothing here for the record."

"What record is that?" Jesse said.

"Don't be smart," she said. "I do not want any notes taken."

"Okay. But I'll probably forget a bunch of stuff," Jesse said, "without notes."

"I want to hear what she has written," Ms. Fiedler said.

"Miriam," Blake said softly.

"No, I insist," Ms. Fiedler said. "What have you written, young woman?"

Molly riffled back though the leaves of her steno pad for a moment, studied a page, and said, "No spicks on Paradise Neck."

Blake looked down. Jesse's face didn't change expression. Ms. Fiedler was horrified.

"How . . . my God in heaven . . . how dare you."

Walter Carr rose to his feet.

"We have said no such thing," he said.

His pinkish face had gotten much pinker. He looked at the lawyer.

"Is this actionable, Austin?"

Blake's face was serious, but Jesse could see the amusement in his eyes.

"Most things are actionable, Walter," he said. "This is not something in which I would expect the action to go your way."

"She has insulted us," Ms. Fiedler said.

"I think she's just kidding you a little, Miriam," Blake said.

"Well, I think she's insulting," Ms. Fiedler said.

She turned on Jesse.

"I want her reprimanded," she said.

"You bet," Jesse said. "How many kids are going to attend this school?"

"Twelve," Carr said.

"So," Jesse said. "A bus will deliver them in the morning and pick them up in the afternoon."

No one answered.

"Twelve of them," Jesse said. "Age?"

"Preschool," Carr said.

Jesse nodded.

"The worst kind," he said.

Carr didn't say anything.

"It is," Ms. Fielder said, "the tip of the camel's nose. It needs to be stopped at the beginning before the value of the Neck simply vanishes."

"Real-estate value?" Jesse said.

"All value," Ms. Fiedler said.

Jesse didn't say anything. The room was silent.

Finally Ms. Fiedler said, "Well?"

"Twelve preschoolers and one bus do not seem to me a public safety issue," Jesse said.

"That's not your decision," Ms. Fiedler said.

"Actually, it is," Jesse said.

"In a democracy," Ms. Fiedler said, "the people rule. You work for us."

"What a terrible thought," Jesse said.

"So you are not going to act?"

"Not at the moment," Jesse said.

Ms. Fiedler stood.

"You have not heard the last of this," she said.

"I was guessing that," Jesse said.

Ms. Fiedler stalked out without speaking again. The men followed her. Carr stared straight ahead. Blake winked at Molly on the way out.

Jesse and Molly sat silently for a time. Then Jesse said, "'No spicks on Paradise Neck'?"

"She was driving me crazy," Molly said.

"I sort of guessed that, too," Jesse said.

"Are you going to reprimand me?" Molly said.

"Worse, I'm going to punish you."

"You are?"

"Yes," Jesse said. "You may not talk dirty to me for the rest of the day."

"Oh, God," Molly said, "not that."

9.

Jesse sat with Suitcase Simpson in the front seat of Simpson's cruiser parked at Paradise Beach. Simpson was eating a submarine sandwich for lunch, taking pains not to dribble on his uniform shirt. Jesse was drinking coffee.

"Funny," Simpson said. "Whenever you're near the ocean, you have to look at it."

Jesse nodded.

"Always makes me feel religious," Simpson said.

Jesse nodded.

"I wonder why that is?" Simpson said.

"Got me," Jesse said.

"Make you feel religious?" Simpson said.

"Yes."

They looked at the ocean for a time. It was high tide and the water covered most of the beach. A few people in bathing suits occupied the narrow strip of sand above high water.

"Crow knows we're watching him," Simpson said.

"No reason he shouldn't," Jesse said. "Who's with him now."

"Eddie."

"Crow doing anything interesting?" Jesse said.

"Nope."

Simpson finished his sandwich and wiped his mouth with a paper napkin. He put the napkin and the sandwich wrappings back in the paper bag that the sandwich had come in.

"Mostly," Simpson said, "he hangs around. He has lunch at Daisy Dyke's a lot. He has a drink at the Gray Gull in the evening. Goes to Paradise Health & Fitness every day in the morning. Rest of the time he cruises around town."

"Walking or driving?" Jesse said.

"Both. Drives all over town. Parks sometimes and walks around. Why?"

"Might help us figure out who or what he's looking for," Jesse said. "Where's he walk around?"

"Shopping center, goes in the stores. Comes to the beach sometimes. Browses all the shops on Paradise Row sometimes. Watches tennis down by the high school."

"He check out the commuter trains?" Jesse said.

Simpson shrugged. He took a small notebook from his shirt pocket and read through it.

"Nope," Simpson said. "Haven't seen him do that. I check

with the other guys, too, and try to incorporate their notes in mine."

Jesse smiled.

"Lead investigator," he said.

"Might as well keep things together," Simpson said. "Do it right, you know?"

"Suit," Jesse said. "If it were in the budget, I'd give you a raise."

"But it's not," Simpson said.

"No. He ever go down to the wharf?" Jesse said.

"Nope."

"Softball?"

"Nope."

"Maybe he's looking for a woman," Jesse said.

"Because of where he looks?"

"Yeah. I know it's a big generalization, but he seems more in-terested in places where you'd find women."

"I don't think you're allowed to think things like that in Paradise," Simpson said.

"Incorrect?" Jesse said.

"This place is officially liberal," Simpson said.

"Long as they keep the cha-chas out," Jesse said.

Simpson smiled.

"Yeah. Molly told me about that."

"Ms. Fiedler was down at the causeway the other day," Jesse said. "With a clicker, counting the number of cars."

"How many kids you say there were?" Simpson said.

"Twelve," Jesse said. "Preschoolers."

"Means a minibus probably," Simpson said. "Once in the morning, and once in the afternoon."

Jesse nodded. They both looked at the blue ocean for a while. Then Simpson grinned.

"They gotta be stopped," Simpson said.

10.

Jesse's ex-wife stuck her head into his office and said, "Hi, Toots, got a minute?"

Jesse felt the small trill of excitement in his belly that he always felt when he saw her.

"I got a minute," he said.

Jenn came in, dressed to the nines, and gave Jesse a pleasant but passing kiss on the mouth. The trill of excitement tightened into a knot of desire and sadness. The kiss was passionless.

"I am on an investigative assignment," Jenn said.

"What's Channel Three investigating this time," Jesse said. "The resurgence of platform soles?"

Jenn smiled.

"Are you saying that Newsbeat Three is not noted for high seriousness?"

"Yes," Jesse said.

"This is a good one for me," Jenn said. "It's like hard news investigation."

Jesse nodded. The knot in his stomach held tight. He knew it would be there until well after she left.

"Our sources tell us that Latino gangs are infiltrating Paradise," Jenn said.

Jesse stared at her.

"Latino gangs," he said.

"There is gang graffiti on several buildings in Paradise," Jenn said.

She took some snapshots out of her purse and put them on Jesse's desk so he could see them.

"Our sources sent us these pictures," Jenn said.

Jesse recognized a couple. One had been on the side of the commuter rail station for more than a year. One had appeared on the back wall of the food market at the mall. There were two more he hadn't seen.

"Can you name your sources?"

Jenn shook her head.

"Does the name Miriam Fiedler mean anything to you?"

She smiled.

"Walter Carr?"

Jenn smiled again but she didn't say anything.

"Jenn," Jesse said. "There has not been a gang-related crime in this town since I've been here."

"Isn't that odd?" Jenn said. "I mean, Marshport is right next door. There are gangs there."

"Several," Jesse said.

"You don't think they might want to slip in here, sometimes, where the streets are paved in gold?"

Jesse leaned back a little in his chair. Jenn had her legs crossed. Her pants were tight. He could see the smooth line of her thigh.

"I never lived in a slum, exactly. But I worked in a lot of them in L.A. People who live in suburbia think every slum dweller yearns to live there, too," Jesse said. "But many people I knew liked the 'hood. Wouldn't want to leave it. Would die of boredom and conformity if they lived elsewhere."

"To me," Jenn said, "that sounds like an excuse to do nothing about slums."

"That's probably it," Jesse said.

"No," Jenn said. "I didn't mean that you were like that. But are you saying none of the gangbangers ever cross the line into Paradise?"

"Oh, they come over sometimes. Mostly, I think, to sell dope to high-school kids."

"Can't you stop them?"

"Can I stop kids from buying dope?" Jesse said.

Jenn nodded.

"Or selling it?" Jesse said.

Jenn nodded again.

"No," Jesse said.

"You can't?"

"No," Jesse said. "But I don't feel too bad about that. Nobody else can, either. Anywhere."

"Are you suggesting we just ignore it?"

Jesse was silent for a moment, looking at her.

Then he said, "Are we on camera?"

"Oh, God, Jesse, I'm sorry. I don't mean to be inquisitorial. I just get so caught up in being Ms. Journalist, you know? Always ask the follow-up question."

Jesse nodded.

"I would like to investigate the gang thing, though," Jenn said.

She smiled. The force of her smile was nearly physical. Jesse always felt as if he should grunt from impact.

"Not a good career move," she said, "to go back and tell the news director that my ex says there's no story."

"No," Jesse said.

"Are you mad 'cause I was, like, cross-examining you?"

"No."

"I care about my job, you know."

"I know."

"It matters to me, just like yours matters to you."

"I know."

"I guess it makes me sort of a pill sometimes," Jenn said.

"Everyone's job corrupts them a little, I imagine," Jesse said. "And you could never be a pill."

Jen smiled at him.

"Even your job?" she said.

Jesse nodded.

"What has your job done to you?" Jenn said.

Jesse was silent for a time.

"I guess," he said finally, "you could say it has narrowed the circle of my expectations."

Jenn stared at him and widened her eyes.

"You want to talk about that?" she said.

"Not much," Jesse said.

"Please," Jenn said. "I'm not being girl reporter now. I'm being ex-wife who still loves you."

Jesse felt the tension he always felt with Jenn: trying to control himself, trying to keep what he felt stored carefully away so it wouldn't spill out all over the place. He flexed his shoulders a little.

"It's pretty hard," Jesse said, "to believe in much. You can't prevent crime. You couldn't even solve most crimes if the bad guys would simply keep their mouths shut. About all you can aim at is to make your corner peaceful."

"But you keep at it," Jenn said.

"Gotta keep at something," Jesse said.

"You see too much of human emotion, up too close," Jenn said. "Don't you? People lie—to you, to themselves. Few people can be counted on. Most people do what they need to do, not what they ought."

"You know that, too," Jesse said.

"I work in television, Jesse."

"Oh," Jesse said. "Yeah."

They were quiet.

Outside Jesse's window a couple of firemen were washing their cars in the broad driveway of the fire station. Jesse could hear the phone ring dimly at the front desk, and Molly's voice.

"So what do we hang on to?' Jenn said.

"Each other?" Jesse said.

"I guess," Jenn said.

"And we're having a hell of a time doing that," Jesse said.

11.

The east side of Marshport butted up against the west side of Paradise. Marshport was an elderly mill town with no mills. There was an enclave of Ukrainians in the southwest end of town. The rest of the city was mostly Hispanic. There had been a couple of feeble efforts to reinvigorate parts of the city, but the efforts had simply replaced the old slums with newer ones.

Jesse parked in front of a building that used to house a grammar school and now served as office space for the few enterprises in Marshport that needed offices. He had driven his own car. He was not in uniform. He was wearing jeans and a white shirt, with a blue blazer over his gun.

The door to Nina Pinero's office had OUTREACH stenciled on

it in black. Jesse went in. The office was a former classroom, on the second floor, in back, with a view of a playground where a couple of kids shot desultory baskets on a blacktop court at a hoop with a chain net. The playground was littered with bottles and newspapers and fast-food wrappers and scraps of indeterminate stuff.

The blackboard was still there, and the bulletin board, which was covered with memos tacked up with colored map pins. There were a couple of file cabinets against the near wall, and Nina Pinero's desk looked like a holdover from the classroom days. There were three telephones on it.

"Nina Pinero?" Jesse said.

"I'm Nina," she said.

There was no one else in the room.

"I'm Jesse Stone," Jesse said. "I called earlier."

"Mr. Stone," Nina said. She nodded at a straight chair next to the desk. "Have a seat."

Jesse sat.

"Tell me about your plans for the Crowne estate in Paradise," Jesse said, "if you would."

"So you can figure out how to prevent us?" Nina Pinero said.

"So we can avoid any incivility," Jesse said.

"Latinos are uncivilized?" Nina Pinero said.

"I was thinking more about the folks in Paradise," Jesse said.

She was slim and strong-looking, as if she worked out. Her hair was short and brushed back. She smiled.

"Excuse my defensiveness," she said.

Jesse nodded.

"I understand you are going to bring in a few kids this summer, to get them started."

She nodded.

"Yes," she said. "A kind of pilot program."

"And later add some more kids?"

"When the school year starts and if things have gone well, maybe."

Jesse nodded.

"Your constituency," she said, "probably has used the camel's-nose-in-the-tent phrase by now."

"They have," Jesse said.

"And traffic," Nina Pinero said.

She was dressed in white pants and a black sleeveless top. Her clothes fit her well.

"That, too," Jesse said.

"You believe them?"

"No. They are fearful that when it's time to sell their home, the prospective buyers will be discouraged by a school full of Hispanic Americans."

"They have, I know, already tried the zoning route," Nina Pinero said.

"Town council tells me there are no zoning limits in Paradise that apply to schools," Jesse said. "There are regulations about what you can put near a school but none about what you can put a school near."

"That's right."

"You've done your homework," Jesse said.

"Yes."

"You have legal advice?"

"I'm a lawyer," she said.

"And yet so young and pretty," Jesse said.

"My only excuse is that I don't make any money at it," she said.

Jesse nodded.

"How old are these kids?" Jesse said.

"Four, five, a couple are six."

"Best and the brightest?" Jesse said.

"Yes."

"How do they feel about breaking trail?" he said.

"Scared," she said.

"But willing?"

"Marshport," Nina Pinero said, "is not a good place to be a kid. Most of them are scared anyway. This way maybe we can save a few of them."

"Not all of them?"

"God, no," Nina Pinero said. "Not even very many of them. But it's better than saving none."

"Sort of like being a cop," Jesse said.

"You do what you can," she said.

They sat quietly for a moment. The room was not air-conditioned, and the windows were open. Jesse could hear the thump of the basketball on the asphalt court.

"You're making your initial run Monday?" Jesse said.

"Yes. Do you expect trouble?"

"Probably not. Do you think the kids would mind if I rode the bus with them?"

"You?"

"Me and one of my officers," Jesse said. "Molly Crane. I'd wear my uniform and polish up my badge."

"You do think there might be trouble."

"Not really," Jesse said. "But there could be a picket or two. I'm thinking about the kids mostly."

"Reassured by your presence?"

"Yes. And Molly's."

"Mostly, they are afraid of policemen," Nina Pinero said.

"Maybe Molly and I can help them get past that," Jesse said.

Nina Pinero nodded thoughtfully.

"Yes," she said. "I can see how you might."

12.

In the Gray Gull, Crow was nursing Johnnie Walker Blue on the rocks at the bar when his cell phone rang. He checked the caller ID, and answered it as he walked outside to talk.

"The kid charged a big television set," a voice said at the other end.

"On your account?" Crow said.

"Yeah. She got one of those satellite cards, you know? Her name's on it, but the bill comes to me."

"Her real name?"

"Yeah."

"She know the bill comes to you?" Crow said.

"Who knows what she knows. Bills been coming to me all

her life. I doubt that she ever thought about who pays. Hell, she may not even know that somebody has to."

Crow smiled in the darkness outside the Gray Gull.

"Where'd she get it," Crow said.

"Place called Images in Marshport, Massachusetts."

"So she is around here," Crow said.

"I told you she would be."

"What kind of TV?" Crow said.

"I wrote it down," the voice said.

It was a soft voice. But there was tension in it, as if it wanted to yell and was being restrained.

"Mitsubishi 517," the voice said. "Fifty-five-inch screen."

"So she didn't carry it away," Crow said.

"Not her," the voice said.

"Maybe they'll tell me where they sent it," Crow said.

"Maybe," the voice said.

The connection broke. Crow folded up his cell phone and put it away. He stood for a moment looking across the parking space toward the harbor.

"When I find her," he said aloud, "then what?"

13.

The small bus was yellow, with school-bus plates. And the usual signage about stopping when the lights were flashing. The driver was a white-haired Hispanic man who spoke too little English to have a conversation. Jesse stood in the exit well beside the driver. Molly sat in back with Nina Pinero. Both Molly and Jesse were in full uniform. Jesse even had on the town-issued chief's hat with braid on the front. The children's clothes were spruced and ironed. The children themselves were very quiet. Jesse could see them swallowing nervously. Several of them kept clearing their throats. And though most of them were dark-skinned, Jesse could see that their faces were pale.

The bus went past Paradise Beach. No one paid any attention.

The kids looked at the hot-dog stand. The bus moved out onto the causeway with the crowded harbor to the left and the open Atlantic to the right. The kids stared out the window. The silence in the bus was palpable. Jesse made no attempt to reassure the kids. He knew how useless that was. Across the causeway, the bus went straight ahead on Sea Street. Past the Paradise Yacht Club. The bus stopped in front of a fieldstone wall that separated a rolling lawn from the street. Across the street there was a white van with a big antenna. On the side it said ACTION NEWS 3. At the top of the lawn was a huge weathered-shingle house. A wide, white driveway wound from behind the house down across the big lawn to the opening in the stone wall, where it joined the street. In the opening, on the driveway, there were maybe twenty adults in varying hues of seersucker and flowered hats. Among them in an on-air summer dress and a big glamorous hat was Jenn. With her was a cameraman in a safari vest.

Nina Pinero stood and walked down to the front of the bus. Molly stayed in the rear. She stopped beside Jesse. Jesse nodded at the driver and he opened the bus doors. Jesse stepped out. The gathered adults stared at him. Walter Carr stood with Miriam Fiedler. They both had pamphlets ready. Jesse wondered who they planned to hand them out to.

"Hello," Jesse said. "I've come to protect you from the invaders."

Carr said, "What?"

"I'm here, with Officer Crane, to see that not one of these small savages attacks you or in any way harms your property," Jesse said.

"There's no need to be caustic, Chief Stone," Miriam Fiedler said. "We are simply trying to maintain the integrity of our property and the safety of our streets."

Jesse nodded at Nina Pinero, and she gently pushed a little boy forward. Jesse took his hand as he stepped from the bus.

"Meet the enemy," Jesse said.

The boy was wearing sandals and khaki shorts, and a snow-white T-shirt. Jesse could feel the stiffness in his hand when he held it.

"His name," Jesse said, "is Roberto Valdez. He was five last week."

Nina gently directed a little girl from the bus. Jesse took her hand as she stepped down. She had on red sneakers with red-and-white striped laces, and white shorts and a white T-shirt.

"This is Isabel Gomez," Jesse said. "She won't be five until later this month."

He could feel Isabel tremble a little as he held her hand.

"Okay, Isabel," Jesse said. "You stand with Roberto, right here, beside the bus, behind me."

"Is this really necessary, Chief Stone?" Miriam Fiedler said.

"Yes, ma'am," Jesse said. "It is."

One by one, the kids emerged from the bus and stood fearfully with Jesse for a moment while he introduced them. Finally they were through. Molly got out of the bus and stood with the kids. Nina Pinero got out and stood beside Jesse.

"Chief Stone," Austin Carr said, "we do not have any animosity toward these children. We would support them, and I mean financially, if they wished to establish a nice school and summer camp in Marshport."

At the top of the driveway, several young men and women in shorts and T-shirts came out of the house and stood, waiting.

"Staff is in place," Nina Pinero said to Jesse.

"Okay," Jesse said. "Follow me, kids."

"This is outrageous," Miriam Fiedler said. "We are not a bunch of rabble to be brushed aside."

"You're not?" Jesse said.

With Nina Pinero and Molly herding the children behind him, Jesse walked straight through the seersucker circle and up the driveway. Behind him he heard Miriam Fiedler cry out in pain.

He heard Molly say, "Oh, dear, I'm so sorry. I seem to have stepped on your foot."

Jesse didn't turn around to look. But he smiled as he led the kids up the driveway.

14.

Wilson Cromartie, in a tan summer suit and a yellow ging-
ham shirt, walked down the center passage of a big mall that had
replaced the nineteenth-century brick buildings in the heart of
Marshport. There were some shoppers, but the majority of the
people in the mall were Hispanic teenagers, in the various cos-
tumes of their age group. A number of them were in a store called
Images, gazing at the television sets they couldn't afford.

Crow went into the store.

"My daughter bought a big-screen TV here a while ago," Crow
said to the clerk. "And the delivery seems to have gone astray."

"Astray?"

"Yes," Crow said. "She never got it."

"Oh, my," the clerk said.

He turned to the computer.

"What's your daughter's name, sir?"

"Amber Francisco," Crow said.

The clerk worked the computer for a moment.

"Twelve-A Horn Street?" the clerk said.

Crow nodded. The clerk smiled.

"It was delivered ten days ago," the clerk said. He was triumphant. "Signed for by Esteban Carty."

Crow looked puzzled.

"Here in Marshport?"

"Yes, sir. If you'd like to step around the counter, I can show you."

"No," Crow said. "Thank you. That'll be fine."

He shook his head.

"Damn kid will put me in an early grave," he said.

He left the store. As he walked back through the mall, several of the teenage girls lounging about watched him as he passed.

15.

Jenn came into the police station with her cameraman, waved at Molly, and came to Jesse's office, the cameraman behind her.

"No cameras in the station," Jesse said when he saw them.

The cameraman looked at Jenn.

"You want to make it a freedom-of-the-press thing?" he said.

Jenn grinned.

"Go ahead, Mike," Jenn said. "Take a break in the van. I'll just talk with Jesse."

The cameraman picked up his camera and went out. Jenn sat across from Jesse.

"Very impressive," she said.

Jesse nodded.

"Riding in with the little kids. Introducing them. Made the protesters look foolish," Jenn said.

Jesse nodded again.

"I kind of liked it also," Jenn said, "when Molly stomped on that woman's foot."

"Molly being Molly," Jesse said.

"I am woman, hear me roar," Jenn said.

"I suspect Molly would be Molly with or without feminism," Jesse said.

Jenn nodded.

"I like her," Jenn said.

"I like her, too," Jesse said.

"What do you suppose the protesters really want in all of this?" Jenn said.

"We on the record here, Jenn?"

"I'd like to be," Jenn said.

Jesse nodded.

"No comment," he said.

Jenn leaned back a little in her chair and looked at Jesse with her head tilted to the side. Her summer dress had slid up to mid-thigh. Her legs were tan. Jesse felt the feeling. He had felt the feeling for such a long time now that it was nearly routine. Sometimes he thought it was the only feeling he had.

"Okay, then," Jenn said. "Off the record."

"First, a question for you," Jesse said. "How'd you happen to be there."

"It's news," Jenn said with a smile. "A lawyer named Blake called us up and informed us of that."

Jesse shook his head.

"They actually think if they get coverage," Jenn said, "they'll get sympathy."

Jesse nodded.

"Maybe a little out of touch," Jesse said. "They probably have a couple of problems with the Crowne estate project. Neither of which, as you may have observed, is traffic."

"Hell," Jenn said. "Our van took up as much space as your bus."

"It did," Jesse said. "One of their problems is they fear a decrease in the value of real estate around the school. And if everybody is like them, the real estate next to a school for disadvantaged children will be harder to sell. And they think that everybody is like them. Or at least everybody who counts."

"They do seem insular," Jenn said.

"Most people are."

"What's their other problem?" Jenn said.

"They don't want a bunch of low-class wetbacks moving into Paradise."

"Simple bigotry?" Jenn said.

"It's almost always that," Jesse said, "when you wipe away the bullshit."

"Wow," Jenn said. "Cynical, cynical, cynical."

"I like to think of it as profiting from the learning experience," Jesse said.

"May I use any of this?"

"No."

"Why not?"

"Because it was off the record," Jesse said. "Feel free to use anything I said on the record."

"The only thing you said on the record was 'no comment.'"

"Feel free," Jesse said.

16.

Mostly Molly ran the front of the police station, but she had persuaded Jesse to allow her, at least once a week, to take a shift on patrol. Jesse had not wanted her shift to be at night. But after Molly explained that he was treating her like a woman, not a cop, and that she was both and should be treated as both, Jesse put her out every couple of weeks, at night, in one of the two patrol cars.

Tonight she was cruising Paradise Neck. She liked the night patrol. Every night would be awful. She'd never see her husband or her kids. But once every couple of weeks it was very soothing. She felt safe enough. Paradise was hardly a war zone. She also had a .40-caliber handgun, Mace, a nightstick, a radio, and the shotgun locked to the dashboard.

She smiled. *Armed to the teeth.*

She passed a pickup truck parked on Ocean Street. *White-collar affectation,* she thought. Riding in the soft darkness, she could think about things like white-collar affectation. She could worry about her children. She could ponder what would become of them. She could think about her husband and herself when the kids had grown. She giggled to herself. She could think about Wilson Cromartie, known as Crow. She shook her head. She had never cheated on her husband. Probably never would. If she did, it would probably be with Jesse, and not an Apache gunman. And even if she wanted to cheat with Jesse, she was not sure he'd allow it. He had so many little rules. *Which,* she said to herself, *is one of the reasons you find him attractive in the first place.*

As she rounded a curve on Ocean Street she saw dimly a man coming down the front walk of one of the big houses that overlooked the Atlantic on the outer side of the Neck. It was 3:10 in the morning. She slowed when she saw him. He paused in the shadow of a shrub and waited. She drove slowly past. Around the next bend she U-turned and drove back. The man was walking back down Ocean Street toward where she'd seen the pickup truck. He was a big man, and his walk looked familiar. She pulled up beside him and looked. Then she pulled ahead and parked and lowered her window.

"Suitcase Simpson," she said. "You get right in this cruiser, right now."

Suitcase said, "Hi, Molly," and got in beside her.

"That your truck up ahead?" Molly said.

"Yep."

"Was that Miriam Fiedler's house you were coming out of when I passed you before and you tried to hide in the bushes?"

"I wasn't hiding," Suitcase said.

"You were, too, and it is Miriam Fiedler's house," Molly said.

Suitcase shrugged.

"You doing some off-duty security work?" Molly said.

Suitcase looked at her and grinned.

"No," he said. "I was banging Mrs. Fiedler."

"Suit," Molly said, "you dog."

Suitcase smiled and nodded.

"Where's Mr. Fiedler?"

"He travels," Suit said, "a lot."

"Weren't you, in your elegant phrase, banging Hasty Hathaway's wife a few years back?"

"I was," Suit said.

"And not embarrassed about it," Molly said.

"She was hot," Suit said.

"And Mrs. Fiedler?" Molly said. "With the teeth?"

"You'd be surprised," Suit said.

"You together often?" Molly said.

"Whenever Mister goes traveling."

"Which is often."

"Often enough," Suitcase said.

"You think there's any conflict of interest here?" Molly said. "We're sort of opposing her efforts to keep the Latinos out of the Crowne estate."

"Sleeping with the enemy?" Suit said.

"You might say that," Molly said.

"We don't talk about the Crowne estate when we're together."

"What do you talk about?"

"Sex stuff," Suit said.

"Jesus," Molly said.

She stopped the cruiser beside Suit's truck.

"You want to hear what she says when we're in bed together?" Suit said.

"Good God, no," Molly said. "I'm already horrified."

"It'll be our secret, though, right, Moll?" Suit said. "Chief might not like it."

"He's nobody to disapprove," she said. "I'm surrounded by a bunch of billy goats."

Suit got out of the cruiser. He leaned his head back in through the open door.

"Mum's the word, Moll?" he said

"Mum," Molly said.

Suit closed the door and got in his truck.

As she drove away, Molly giggled.

"Miriam Fiedler," she said aloud. "Oh, my sweet Jesus."

17.

The sun shining through the window made a long, bright splash on the far wall of Dix's office. Dix was at his desk. As always, he was immaculate. His white shirt gleamed. His bald head shone. The crease in his gray slacks could have been used to sharpen pencils. His cordovan loafers gleamed darkly.

"Why do you suppose she's like that?" Jesse said to Dix.

"Sounds as if her career matters to her," Dix said.

"More than I do," Jesse said.

Dix shrugged.

"She's still pursuing the career," he said.

"And not me," Jesse said.

"Is that true?" Dix said.

"No," Jesse said. "She does still pursue me."

Dix nodded. The air-conditioning made its quiet sound.

"Maybe she wants both," Dix said.

"I don't see why they'd be mutually exclusive," Jesse said.

Dix was quiet. It was always amazing to Jesse how still Dix could be, and yet how clearly his stillness could speak. Jesse knew that in the language of psychotherapy, Dix was asking him to examine that issue.

"Do you?" Jesse said.

"I only know what you tell me," Dix said.

"The hell you do," Jesse said.

"I only know about you and about Jenn by listening to what you tell me about you and about Jenn."

"And bringing to bear thirty years of training and experience to interpret what you heard," Jesse said.

Dix smiled and tipped his head in acceptance.

"We won't divert ourselves with the difference between knowing and interpreting," Dix said. "Let's just agree that my innocence is a fiction that is useful to the process."

"Okay," Jesse said. "What you know, if you're a cop, is that what people say needs to be compared to what they do."

Dix seemed to nod.

"So," Jesse said, "Jenn left me to pursue her career but never quite let go, and has ricocheted between me and her career ever since."

"What do you suppose her career represents to her?" Dix said.

"Represents?"

Dix again almost nodded.

"Sometimes," Jesse said, "a cigar is just a cigar."

Dix smiled.

"And sometimes it's not," Dix said.

They were quiet. The sunsplash on the wall had become longer.

"She started out trying to be an actress," Jesse said, "and kind of morphed into a weather girl."

"In California?" Dix said.

"No," Jesse said. "Here."

Dix nodded.

"I assume she came here because I was here," Jesse said.

Dix nodded again.

"And then she morphed into a soft-feature reporter," Jesse said. "She did a special on Race Week, few years ago."

Dix waited.

"And then she sort of morphed into an investigative reporter when we had the big murder case last year."

"Walton Weeks," Dix said. "National news. How'd she draw that assignment?"

"Probably because she was my ex-wife," Jesse said. "They figured it would give her access."

"Did it?"

"Some," Jesse said.

Dix waited.

"So I'm kind of tangled up in her career," Jesse said.

Dix waited.

"And sometimes she exploits me," Jesse said.

Dix didn't move.

"And sometimes," Jesse said, "it's like she compromises her career because of me."

Dix made no sign. Jesse didn't say anything else for a while.

Then he said, "So her career and me are clearly tied together in some way."

Dix looked interested. Jesse was silent again. Then he looked at Dix and spread his hands.

"So what?" he said. "I don't know where to go with it."

Dix was quiet for a long time. Then he apparently decided to prime the pump.

"What's your career mean to you?" Dix said.

"Redemption," Jesse said. "We already settled that in here."

"Uh-huh."

"Redemption for being a drunk and a lousy husband..." Jesse said.

"And for getting hurt," Dix said, "and washing out of baseball?"

"Yeah, that, too."

"Being a good cop is your chance," Dix said.

"To be good at something," Jesse said. "I know, we already talked about that."

They were quiet again. Jesse had done this long enough to know that the fifty minutes were almost up.

"You think her career is her chance at redemption?" Jesse said.

"I don't know," Dix said. "What do you think?"

"Weather girl isn't much of a redemption," Jesse said.

"How about investigative reporter?"

Jesse nodded.

"I just demeaned her a little, didn't I," he said.

Dix didn't answer.

"I must be madder at her than I know," Jesse said.

"Almost certainly," Dix said.

"You think she's after redemption?" Jesse said.

Dix looked at his watch, as he always did before closing the session.

"We'll have time to think about that on our own," Dix said. "Until next time. Time's up for today."

"Hell," Jesse said. "Just when it was getting good."

18.

Crow stood in front of a three-decker on an unpaved street
that was little more than old wheel ruts overgrown with stiff,
gray-green weeds. There were tenements on either side of the rut-
ted street, the paint long peeled, the clapboards gray and warped
with weather. A street sign nailed to one of the tenements read
HORN STREET. Crow walked down to a sagging three-decker that
blocked the end of the street. Over the skewed front door was a
number 12.

A small path that might once have been a driveway ran around
the tenement and Crow followed it, walking carefully to avoid the
beer cans, fast-food cartons, dog droppings, used condoms, dis-

carded tires, bottles, rusted bicycle parts, and odd bits of clothing and bedding that were strewn outside the building. Behind the tenement was a metal garage, which had been repainted without being scraped. The bright yellow finish was lumpy and uneven. The maroon trim, Crow noticed, had been applied freehand and not very precisely. A window in the side of the garage had a window box haphazardly affixed below it. The box was filled with artificial flowers. The garage door was ajar. Above the garage door was the number 12A.

Crow went through the half-open door into the garage.

Inside, there were six young men and a huge rear-projection television set. The young men were drinking beer and watching a soap opera. When Crow stepped into the garage they all came to their feet.

"Who the fuck are you," one of them said.

"I'm looking for Esteban Carty," Crow said.

"And I said who the fuck are you?"

"My name is Wilson Cromartie," Crow said. "You Carty?"

"You ain't a cop."

The speaker was short, with shoulder-length black hair and a full beard. He was wearing a tank top and there were gang tattoos up each arm.

"Cops don't come in here alone," he said.

"I'm still looking for Esteban Carty," Crow said. "And I'm getting tired of asking."

"Hey, Puerco," the long-haired kid said. "Wilson getting tired of asking."

Puerco was big, with a shaved head, weight-lifter muscles, no shirt, and a round, hard belly. His upper body was covered with tattoos, including one across his forehead: PUERCO.

Puerco stared at Crow. He had very small eyes for so large a man. There was something else peculiar about his eyes, Crow thought. Then he realized that Puerco had no eyebrows. Crow wondered if it was a defect of nature, or if Puerco had shaved them so as to look more baleful.

"Getting tired of Wilson," Puerco said.

"People do," Crow said.

"Throw him the fuck out," the long-haired kid said.

"Sí, Esteban," Puerco said.

"Okay," Crow said, "you're Carty. I'm looking for Amber Francisco."

Puerco stepped across the room toward Crow. Without appearing even to look at him, Crow hit him with the edge of his right hand on the upper lip directly below the nose. Puerco screamed. It was so explosive that none of the others had time to react before Crow had a gun out and pointed at them. Puerco went down, doubled up on the floor, his face buried in his hands, moaning.

"So," Crow said. "Where do I find Amber Francisco."

"I don't know nobody named Amber Francisco," Carty said.

"Girl who bought you the television," Crow said. "What's her name?"

"No bitch bought me nothing," Carty said.

Crow lowered the gun and shot Puerco through the head as he lay moaning on the floor.

Esteban Carty said, "Jesus."

No one else spoke or moved. Crow pointed the gun at Esteban Carty.

"Amber Francisco?" Crow said.

"Bitch bought me the TV name is Alice," Esteban said, "Alice Franklin."

"Where's she live?" Crow said.

"She lives in Paradise, man, her and her old lady."

"Thank you," Crow said. "I'll kill anybody comes out this door while I'm in sight."

Then he stepped through the door and walked away through the trash, toward the street.

19.

Molly came into Jesse's office with Miriam Fiedler right behind her. Molly stopped in the doorway, blocking Miriam Fiedler
from entering.

Molly said, "Ms. Fiedler to see you, Jesse."

There was a glitter of amusement in Molly's eyes.

"Show her in," Jesse said. "You stay, too."

Molly stepped aside and Miriam Fiedler brushed past her
angrily.

"This woman is deliberately annoying," she said.

"I doubt that it's deliberate," Jesse said. "Probably can't help it.
Probably genetic."

"I find her impertinent," Miriam Fiedler said.

"Me, too," Jesse said.

Molly sat down to the right of Miriam Fiedler and behind her.

"Is she going to stay here during our meeting?" Miriam said.

"Yes," Jesse said.

"I don't want her here," Miriam said.

Jesse nodded. Miriam waited. Jesse didn't speak.

"Are you going to send her out?" Miriam said.

"No," Jesse said.

"Chief Stone," Miriam said, "may I remind you that I am a resident of this town, and as such am, in fact, your employer?"

"You may remind me of that," Jesse said.

"Are you being sarcastic?" Miriam said.

"Yes," Jesse said.

"I find it offensive," Miriam said.

"Ms. Fiedler," Jesse said, "it is standard practice in this office that Officer Crane be present when a woman is alone with any male police officers. She will stay as long as you are here."

"Well, it's a stupid rule," Miriam said.

"Did you come to berate me?" Jesse said. "Or have you something substantive?"

"I wish to report several instances of Hispanic gang infiltration of Paradise," she said. "Ever since that school was established on Paradise Neck..."

Jesse nodded.

"Specifically?" he said.

"Specifically," Miriam said, "I have recently seen several Hispanic gang members on the street in downtown Paradise."

"How recently," Jesse said.

"In the last two days."

"And how did you know they were Hispanic gang members."

"Well, my dear man," Miriam said, "you can tell just looking."

"What did they look like?" Jesse said.

"Dark, tattoos, one of them was wearing some sort of hairnet."

"Dead giveaway," Jesse said. "How many did you see."

"Two one day," Miriam said. "And three yesterday, walking side by side, so that they took up the whole sidewalk."

"Did they do anything illegal?" Jesse said.

"Well, they weren't here to sightsee," Miriam said.

"But you are not actually reporting a crime?" Jesse said.

"The press is investigating this, too," Miriam said.

"I heard," Jesse said. "Have they uncovered a crime?"

"Take that attitude if you wish," Miriam said. "When they hurt someone, then you'll act?"

"We'll keep an eye out," Jesse said.

"Maybe you can put Officer Simpson on the case," Molly said. "Any assignment he has, he's on top of it."

Miriam Fiedler turned her head involuntarily to stare at Molly. Jesse saw it. He glanced at Molly. She was smiling sweetly at Miriam Fiedler. Jesse decided to look into the remark later.

"I am not empowered by law to run someone out of town," Jesse said. "I wish I were. But we'll be on the lookout."

"Those children," Miriam said. "They are the camel's nose under the tent."

"And it's a slippery slope from there, I imagine," Jesse said.

"Perhaps I should take my story to the media," Miriam said.

"Perhaps you already have," Jesse said.

"I beg your pardon?"

Jesse waved his hand.

"Well, whether I have or not," Miriam said, "I certainly shall. And I expect a more sympathetic hearing than I get from you."

"They are permitted to deal in allegation and innuendo," Jesse said. "I am not."

"I know what I saw," Miriam said.

"We both do," Jesse said. "Molly, could you show Ms. Fiedler out, please."

20.

Crow sat in his rental car parked on a curb in the old town section of Paradise, where the houses crowded against the sidewalk. He had circled the block for more than an hour before a spot had opened up within view of the narrow old house on Sewall Street where Mrs. Franklin lived with her daughter. He sipped some coffee from a big paper cup. He wasn't impatient. He had all the time necessary. No hurry. Crow couldn't really remember ever being in a hurry.

A little after two in the afternoon, a big woman with a lot of coal-black hair came out of the house and started up the street. Her hair was a black that no Caucasian woman could achieve without chemical help. She probably wasn't quite as heavy as she looked, but her breasts were so ponderous that they enlarged her. She wore large harlequin sunglasses.

Crow took a photograph from his inside pocket and looked at it and then at the woman. *Could be.* She passed the car barely three feet from Crow. Up close, her face was puffy and reddish. She wore too much makeup, badly applied. She would be older now, and, of course, the picture was a glamour shot, designed to make her look as good as she could. She was blonde in the picture. But that was easily changed. *Probably her.*

Crow made no move to follow her. He simply sat. In about twenty minutes she came back carrying a paper bag. As she passed the car, Crow could see that the bag contained two six-packs of beer. She went back into her house and closed the door behind her. Crow sat. At about 3:50 the front door opened again and a girl came out. She, too, had very black hair. But hers had a candy-apple-red stripe in it. She used black lipstick and a lot of black makeup around her eyes. She had on a mesh tank top and cutoff denim shorts and black cowboy boots with a red dragon worked into the leather.

Crow took out another picture and looked at it. It was a school picture taken several years ago. Again, the hair color had changed. The makeup was different. She was older. But it was probably Amber Francisco, aka Alice Franklin. She passed Crow heading in the same direction as her mother had, toward Paradise Square. After she passed, he watched her in the rearview mirror. At the top of Sewall Street she met three kids on the corner. They were three of the survivors from 12A Horn Street. One of them was Esteban Carty. The girl and the three men went around the corner. Crow tapped "shave and a haircut, two bits" on the tops of his thighs for a moment. Then he took a cell phone out of the center console and punched up a number.

"I found her," he said. "Her and her mother. But in a couple minutes she's going to know I found her. How you want me to handle it."

"How's she look," the voice said at the other end of the connection.

"The kid?" Crow said.

"Of course the kid, I don't give a fuck how Fiona looks."

Crow smiled but kept the smile out of his voice.

"Looks fine," he said.

"She pretty?"

"Sure," Crow said.

"She's fourteen now, sometimes they change."

"She looks great," Crow said.

"Fiona know about you?"

"Not yet. I assume the kid will tell her," Crow said.

"She might. She might not. Can't take the chance. Kill Fiona and bring me the kid."

Crow took the cell phone from his ear for a moment and looked at it. Then he put it back and spoke into it.

"Sure," he said, and folded shut his cell phone and sat where he was.

21.

"You guys reestablish contact with Crow yet?" Jesse said.

He was in the squad room with Suitcase Simpson, Arthur Angstrom, Peter Perkins, and Molly.

"He knows he's being tailed," Suit said. "He loses us whenever he wants to. You know that."

"I know," Jesse said. "Just asking."

"We been staking out his house," Arthur said. "Figure he'll show up there pretty soon."

"Got a notice out on his car?" Jesse said.

"Car's at the house," Arthur said.

"Maybe he's got another one," Jesse said.

"Another one?"

"Leave the car at home," Jesse said. "Take a cab, rent another car. Cops don't have your number."

"If he can spend that kind of dough," Angstrom said.

Arthur was defensive by nature.

"Arthur," Molly said. "This guy left here ten years ago with about twenty million dollars in cash."

"He's got that kind of dough, why's he here working?" Angstrom said.

"Maybe likes the work," Suit said.

"Maybe he owes a guy a favor," Perkins said.

"Maybe he blew the twenty million," Angstrom said.

Jesse shook his head.

"No," he said. "Crow didn't blow the twenty million."

"How do you know," Arthur said.

"He wouldn't," Jesse said. "Why don't you call around to some local rental agencies, see if he rented a car."

"Maybe he didn't use his real name," Arthur said. "Maybe got himself a whole phony ID."

"Maybe," Jesse said.

"But you want me to call."

"I do," Jesse said.

He looked around the squad room.

"Anything else?"

"You still want a cruiser at the Crowne estate when the buses arrive," Molly said.

"Yep."

"Arrival and pickup?"

"Yep."

"That'd be you this morning, Peter," Molly said.

Perkins nodded.

"Anything else?" Jesse said.

No one spoke.

"Okay," Jesse said. "Go to work."

The cops got up and started out.

"Moll," Jesse said. "Could you stick here a minute?"

Molly sat back down.

When the others had left, Jesse said, "Something going on with Suit and Miriam Fiedler?"

"No," Molly said. "Why?"

"The little joke about Officer Simpson being on top of things."

"I was just teasing her," Molly said. "You know I can't stand her."

"Who can," Jesse said.

Molly didn't say anything. Jesse leaned back and stretched his neck a little, looking up at the ceiling.

"I think there's more, Moll," he said after a time.

"More what?"

"I think there's something between Suit and Miriam Fiedler," Jesse said, "that you have probably promised Suit not to tell me about."

"Honestly, Jesse..." Molly said.

Jesse put up a hand as if he were stopping traffic.

"I don't want to put you in the position where you have to break a promise or lie to me. I like you too much. Hell, I depend on you too much."

"Jesse, I..."

Again, Jesse stopped her.

"Suit is very appealing to a certain kind of older, affluent, dissatisfied woman," Jesse said. "They see him as both masculine and cute. Like a big, friendly bear, and he is often in marked contrast to their husbands."

"Like Hasty Hathaway's wife," Molly said.

"Yeah," Jesse said. "Like her. In return, Suit is flattered by the attention of such a woman, and their age and status seem not to be a detriment but an attraction."

"Oedipus again?" Molly said. "Maybe you've been seeing that shrink too long, Jesse."

"In fact," Jesse said, "not long enough. But for whatever reason, Suit has a track record of bopping some surprising women."

"Lot of that going around," Molly said.

Jesse grinned.

"You bet," Jesse said. "And I'm all for it. As long as it does not compromise what we do here."

"You think Suit is doing the hokey-pokey with Miriam Fiedler?" Molly said.

"I do," Jesse said.

"If you were right, would it harm the department?"

"Not if Suit kept it separate," Jesse said. "Not as long as he continues to serve and protect the kids at the Crowne estate."

"You think he wouldn't?" Molly said.

"No," Jesse said. "I think he will. But I don't want him, or us, embarrassed."

Molly nodded.

"I would," she said, "if he were doing something."

"Good," Jesse said.

They sat together for another moment in silence. Then Jesse looked at Molly and said, "Miriam Fiedler?"

And Molly giggled.

22.

It took a long time for Mrs. Franklin to open the door.

When she did, Crow said, "My name is Wilson Cromartie. I work for a man named Francisco."

She tried to shut the door, but Crow wouldn't let her.

"We need to talk," he said, and forced the door open and went in and closed it behind him.

The woman backed away.

"Don't hurt me," she said.

Her voice was blurred and Crow assumed she'd drunk most of the beer she'd bought earlier.

"I won't hurt you," Crow said.

"He sent you," she said.

"He did. He wants his daughter back."

"He fucking deserves her," the woman said. "How'd you find us."

"Your daughter used a credit card in her own name."

"Dumb bitch," the woman said.

There was an open can of beer on the coffee table in front of the couch. The woman picked it up and drank some.

"He can have her back," the woman said. "I can't do anything with her. But I'm not going back."

"He doesn't want you back," Crow said.

The woman belched softly.

"Good," she said. "'Cause I ain't going."

"He told me to kill you," Crow said.

The woman backed up a step.

"You said you wasn't going to hurt me," she said.

"I'm not," Crow said. "I don't kill women."

"He know that?"

"No."

"What are you doing here?"

"Your daughter's got a boyfriend?"

The woman finished her beer.

"Everybody's her boyfriend, the little slut. Who's she with now?"

"Kid from Marshport named Esteban Carty," Crow said.

"The fucking gangbanger," the woman said.

"Yep."

"She loves those gangbangers," the woman said. "I think she does it to spite me."

Crow nodded. The woman went to the refrigerator and got another beer. While she had the door open, she counted the number of beer cans left.

"I done everything for her, give up everything. Took her away from him. Run off, risked my life taking her with me, so I wouldn't leave her with him. And she comes here and turns into a fucking slut."

"Your daughter's boyfriend knows I found you," Crow said. "She's with him now. So she'll know, too."

"Yeah?"

"I don't want her running off again."

"You think I can stop her?"

"Doesn't matter," Crow said. "I can."

23.

Jenn sat across from Jesse in the Gray Gull, at the window overlooking the harbor. He was sipping a scotch and soda. Jenn had a mojito.

"You're working," Jesse said.

"Why do you think so?"

"You're on expenses," Jesse said, "or you wouldn't have promised to pay for dinner."

Jenn smiled.

"I missed you," she said. "I wanted to talk. You can pay if you'd rather."

"That's okay," Jesse said.

"Secure in your manhood?"

"Something like that," Jesse said.

"I need a favor."

"Sure."

"We have been all over the gang infiltration story," Jenn said. "And I'm not so sure there is a story."

Jesse nodded.

"We keep getting information from a group called Paradise Preserved about gang activity here. But we can't verify much more than a couple of instances of graffiti."

Jesse nodded.

"Are we being jerked around?" Jenn said.

"You are," Jesse said.

"What do they want?"

"They want the Crowne estate project to fail," Jesse said.

"So they are trying to convince people in Paradise that gang invasion is a collateral result?"

"Something like that," Jesse said.

"I suppose it's better than being opposed to education of the young," Jenn said.

"They've discovered, I think, that intimidating five-year-old kids doesn't look good on TV," Jesse said.

"When we talked about this before, I thought you were being defensive and you thought I was being careerist."

"Neither of us was entirely wrong," Jesse said.

Jesse's first drink had been a very small drink. Jenn still had half of hers. His drinking always bothered her. What would she think if he ordered another one? They were divorced and she was sleeping with other men. How much did he have to lose? He gestured toward the waitress.

"No," Jenn said. "I am a careerist, I guess. My job means a great deal to me. As yours does to you."

"I'm good at it," Jesse said. "If I can keep being good at it, maybe I'll get to be good at other things."

"You're good at a lot of things, Jesse."

"Marriage doesn't seem to be one of them," Jesse said.

Jenn shook her head.

"It takes two," Jenn said. "Not to tango."

Jesse smiled.

"I never said you were perfect," he said.

"The mess we're in," Jenn said, "is a collaborative effort. No one person could have created it alone."

Jesse tried to nurse his second drink.

I'll take a sip, he thought, *and put the glass down. And savor the sip. And talk a little. Like Jenn does. And have another sip. No hurry.*

"You're sure there's no story, then," Jenn said.

"Not the one you came out here for," Jesse said.

Jenn had started to pick up the menu. She stopped, her hand resting on it.

"But there is a story," she said.

Jesse sipped some scotch and put the glass back down carefully on the table. He let the drink ease down his throat.

"The Crowne estate project might make an interesting feature piece," Jesse said.

"Yes!" Jenn said. "My God, yes! The conflict between privilege and poverty. Between real-estate values and human values. It could become a…" She moved her hands in circles while she searched for a word. "It could become a replica…a…ah…a microcosm of the same kind of conflict between haves and have-nots worldwide."

"Wow!" Jesse said.

"It's great," Jenn said. "I can sell this, I can sell this."

"How 'bout the conflict between you and me," Jesse said.

"I haven't quit on that," Jenn said.

"Me either," Jesse said.

Jenn picked up his hand in both of hers and looked at his face.

"I have always loved you," she said. "I love you now."

Jesse smiled.

"But right now you have a story to sell," he said.

"Yes, I do," Jenn said. "And don't dismiss it, Jesse, it might be my way back."

"To what?" Jesse said.

"To you, for crissake, don't you see that? To you."

24.

The woman was on the couch with a half-drunk can of beer on the coffee table in front of her. Her head was tilted back against the top of the couch. Her mouth had fallen open. She was snoring gently. Crow sat across the room. If someone opened the door, Crow would be out of sight behind it. At 11:07 the daughter arrived.

"Ma," she said, and saw her mother slumped on the couch. "Oh, swell," she said. "Have another beer, Ma."

She closed the door and saw Crow.

"Shit!" she said.

Crow smiled at her.

"Should I come back later?" the daughter said. "Or did you fuck her already."

"No need to come back later," Crow said.

The woman on the couch came awake with a startle.

"Alice?"

"I think Daddy's found us," Alice said. "Esteban told me a guy..."

She stopped and looked at Crow.

"You're the guy."

"That visited Esteban?"

"Yes."

"I am," Crow said.

"You shot Puerco," Alice said.

"Only once," Crow said.

"Shot?" the mother said.

"Shut up, Ma," Alice said. "He works for Daddy."

Mrs. Franklin frowned, trying to focus.

"He said he wasn't gonna hurt us," she said.

"Whaddya gonna do?" Alice said.

"Your old man asked me to kill your mother and bring you back to him."

"Kill her," Alice said.

"Yeah."

"And bring me back?" Alice said.

"Yeah."

"You gonna do either one?"

Crow shook his head.

"So whaddya gonna do?"

"I don't know," Crow said. "You got any suggestions?"

"Whyn't you go kill Daddy," she said.

Crow nodded.

"And what would you do then?" he said.

"What I'm gonna do anyway. Move in with Esteban."

"Not on your life," her mother said. "I didn't raise you to slut for no spick gangbanger."

"You didn't raise me at all, you fucking drunk," Alice said. "I go where I want. I want to slut it up with Esteban, you got no say."

"Don't you talk to me that way," her mother said, and struggled to get off the couch.

"You calling me a slut," Alice said. "There's a laugh."

"I rescued you from your father, and you talk to me like this?"

"At least I'm not a fat slut," Alice said. "I'm outta here."

She turned and found Crow standing in front of the door.

"Get the fuck out of my way," she said.

Crow slapped her hard across the face and sent her halfway across the room. She fell back onto the couch beside her mother and began to cry with her face buried in her hands.

"Esteban is going to kill you," she said. "He's going to kill you for Puerco, and now, when I tell him, he'll kill you for me, too."

Crow took his cell phone out and punched in a number.

After a moment he said, "Chief Stone? Wilson Cromartie. We got a situation down here on Sewall Street."

25.

Jesse brought Molly with him. They were all together in the living room. Jesse standing by the door. Molly in the opposite corner so Crow wouldn't be able to shoot them both together. Crow sat on a reversed straight chair, his arms folded across the back. Alice's face was red from Crow's slap, and her heavy black eye makeup had run when she cried.

"Can we talk off the record?" Crow said.

"I don't see why we should," Jesse said.

"Guy named Louis Francisco," Crow said. "Lives in Palm Beach. Does business all over South Florida. He's very, very important in South Florida. Miami, all over. He's married to this woman, calls herself Frances Franklin, but her real name's Fiona.

Fiona Francisco. Kid here, looks kind of like Alice Cooper, is his daughter. She goes by Alice Franklin around here. But her real name's Amber Francisco."

Jesse didn't comment. He waited, leaning on the wall, his arms folded across his chest. In the opposite corner, Molly was watching both women as Crow talked.

"One day, about three years ago, in the middle of the afternoon, Mrs. Francisco"—Crow nodded toward her—"and the kid disappear. Francisco's upset. He don't care too much about Fiona. But he wants the kid."

Crow paused for a moment, thinking about what he'd say next. No one else said anything.

"So," Crow said, "think about it. You're Louis Francisco. You don't know where your daughter is. And you don't know who's got her, or so you say. But you not only want her back but you probably want to get her away from her mother, whom you consider a bad influence."

"He should talk," Fiona Francisco said.

No one paid her any attention.

"What do you do?" Crow said. "You probably hire somebody to find her. Now suppose he did, hypothetically, hire somebody. And suppose the guy found them. And he calls Louis and tells him and Louis says kill the mother, bring the girl to me."

"He would say that," Fiona said. "The prick."

"I'm not going back," Amber Francisco said.

"And here's the kicker," Crow said. "This hypothetical guy doesn't want to do it. He doesn't want to kill the mother and he doesn't want to drag the daughter down to Florida."

"Why?" Jesse said.

"Guy's got his reasons," Crow said. "But hypothetically, he's already annoyed the hell out of the members of a Latino gang in Marshport. And Louis won't be too thrilled with this hypothetical guy, who took a lot of dough up front from Louis and is now not doing what he was signed up for."

"So why doesn't our hypothetical friend tuck his hypothetical ass under him and scoot?" Jesse said.

"Probably wouldn't be his style," Crow said.

"And he doesn't quite want to bail on these women," Jesse said.

"Something like that," Crow said. "If he was an actual guy."

Jesse was nodding his head slowly. Crow waited.

"Okay," Jesse said. "I can't stand this hypothetical crap anymore. We're off the record."

"Which means?" Crow said.

"Which means I won't use anything you say against you," Jesse said.

Crow looked at him for a time.

"Good," Crow said.

"So you got Louis Francisco on your ass," Jesse said, "and I assume he has a lot of resources for getting on your ass."

"He does," Crow said. "On the other hand, I got kind of a hard ass."

From across the room, Molly said, "Uh-huh!"

Crow looked at her and grinned.

"And," Jesse said, "you got a Latino gang on your ass for a reason not yet specified."

"Correct."

"And you want me to keep track of these women while you deal with your other problems."

"Correct."

Jesse was quiet for a moment.

Then he said, "What's in this for me?"

"Do the right thing?" Crow said.

Jesse stared at him.

"Crow," Jesse said, "how many people you killed in your life?"

"It's bush to count," Crow said.

"And you think I'll do it because it's the right thing to do?"

"Yeah."

"What makes you so sure."

"It's the way you are," Crow said.

"How the hell do you know the way I am?" Jesse said.

"I know," Crow said.

Again, a pause.

Then Jesse said, "Yeah, you probably do."

26.

"I can't hold them for long," Jesse said.

He and Crow were in his office. The Francisco women, mother and daughter, were in the squad room with Molly and Suitcase Simpson.

"Part of a criminal conspiracy?" Crow said.

"I don't think that statute covers the intended victims," Jesse said.

"At least you could put a cop with them," Crow said.

"Yeah," Jesse said. "I can. And I will. But if either or both decides to run off, my cop can't stop them."

"You got them now," Crow said.

"For questioning. They can leave when they want to."

Crow didn't say anything.

"Why do you care about any of this?" Jesse said.

"Why not?" Crow said.

"Why'd you take the job in the first place? You need the money?"

"Hell, no," Crow said. "I came into a lot of money, 'bout ten years ago."

"So...?"

"Being rich can get boring," Crow said. "I like to work. Francisco leads me to think there might be some push and shove when I found the women. He led me to believe that somebody might be with them that would need to be..." Crow made a small rolling gesture with his right hand. "Removed."

"And that would be your kind of work."

"It would," Crow said. "I'm very good at it."

"So you took the job because you wanted to get into it with somebody?" Jesse said.

Crow shrugged.

"No point being a warrior if you can't find a war," he said.

Jesse stared at him.

"Warrior?" Jesse said.

"I am a full-blooded Apache warrior," Crow said.

Jesse looked at him for a sign that he was joking. There was no sign.

"And warriors don't go to war against women and girls," Jesse said.

"No," Crow said, "they don't."

"That's why you let those women hostages go, ten years ago," Jesse said, "off the boat."

"I like women," Crow said.

"If the money had been on shore with Macklin," Jesse said, "would you still have let them go?"

Crow smiled.

"Can't go back and do it different," Crow said.

Jesse nodded. Crow was silent again.

"So how come you decided to look for the Francisco women here?" Jesse said.

"Francisco said he thought they'd be here."

"He say why?"

"Nope."

"You ask?"

"Nope."

"So how'd you find them?" Jesse said.

"Kid charged a big TV set for her boyfriend on one of those satellite credit cards, you know, bill goes to Daddy. Daddy calls me and I run it down. Thing was too big to carry. It was delivered to a gang house in Marshport."

"So you went there," Jesse said.

"Yep."

"Alone."

"Yep."

"How'd you get them to tell you where she was?"

"I had to shoot one of them," Crow said. "Their bad man, guy named Puerco."

"Pig," Jesse said.

"You speak Spanish?"

"Used to work in L.A.," Jesse said. "Had some time in Boyle Heights. Self-defense?"

"Of course."

"What gang?" Jesse said.

"Never mentioned their name."

"Where were they?" Jesse said.

"Dump at the end of an alley called Horn Street. Twelve-A Horn Street."

"Horn Street Boys," Jesse said.

"You know the gangs in Marshport?"

"Like to keep up," Jesse said.

Molly came into the office.

"The women are asking for a lawyer," she said.

Crow studied her.

"Tell them that they can go after they talk with one more cop," Jesse said.

"Who?"

"Who's on the desk?"

"Peter Perkins," Molly said.

"Okay," Jesse said. "Send Suit out front. Tell Peter to ask them anything he can think of."

"Peter doesn't know the case," Molly said. "He doesn't even know their names."

"Doesn't matter."

"We don't get them a lawyer when they ask, any case we bring into court gets tossed."

"Doesn't matter," Jesse said. "We're not bringing a case against them."

"We're just stalling," Crow said, "until we figure out what to do."

Molly turned and looked straight at Crow.

"We?" Molly said.

Crow smiled at her.

"So to speak," he said.

Molly smiled back, and turned and left. Crow watched her go. Jesse was pretty sure she was swinging her hips more than she normally did.

Jesse said, "What do you want out of all this, Crow?"

"I want these two broads to be okay, and have that be my doing."

"Because?"

"I told you," Crow said, "I like women."

"Or you don't," Jesse said.

"Don't?"

"Because they aren't worthy opponents," Jesse said.

Crow shrugged.

"What do you think of the men in their lives?" Jesse said.

"Don't like them. Don't like Francisco. Don't like the gangbanger."

"Because?"

"Because the gangbanger's a punk," Crow said. "And Francisco is a liar."

"You ever wonder why he hired somebody like you to find his daughter?"

"I figured he might want somebody killed along the way."

"And you were willing."

"I was willing to take his money and see what developed," Crow said. "I'm not willing to kill a couple women."

"For the moment," Jesse said.

Crow shrugged.

"'Course, the daughter could turn out to be some sort of hole card for you," Jesse said.

"Could," Crow said.

"You think the mother would abandon her daughter?" Jesse said.

"They do sometimes," Crow said.

"I know," Jesse said. "But often they don't. Maybe we let them go, what happens. Kid isn't going to leave the boyfriend. Mother isn't going to leave the kid. Boyfriend's not going anywhere. Most gang kids never leave the neighborhood until they go to jail."

"Yeah?"

"So they stay right here while I figure out what to do about a couple things," Jesse said.

"Like what?"

"Like how to help them, and what the hell you're up to."

"What if she moves in with him?" Crow said.

"We know where she is," Jesse said.

"Not much of a life on Horn Street," Crow said.

"Not much of a life on Sewall Street, either," Jesse said.

"There's bad and there's worse," Crow said.

"Won't be forever," Jesse said. "Once I get it figured out, we'll go take her away from Horn Street."

"And if she won't come?" Crow said.

"We make her."

"Man, you are cold," Crow said.

"Keep it in mind," Jesse said.

"How come you're going along with any of this?" Crow said.

"Girl's a mess," Jesse said. "Her old man is in the rackets in South Florida..."

"Her old man *is* the rackets in South Florida," Crow said.

"...and her mother's a drunk," Jesse continued. "Kid needs help. And you seem like you might give her some."

Crow nodded.

"Okay," Crow said.

"Let's be clear," Jesse said. "I don't trust you."

"Be crazy if you did," Crow said.

"I don't believe this is pure concern for the Francisco girls," Jesse said.

Crow shrugged.

"Don't matter too much what you believe," Crow said. "Thing you can trust, though. I keep my word."

Jesse nodded.

"And you keep yours," Crow said.

"You think?"

"I know you, Stone, just like you know me. We been listening to the same music for a long time."

"And we know all the lyrics?" Jesse said.

"All the ones that matter," Crow said.

27.

Jesse invited Nina Pinero to lunch.

"In Marshport?" she said. "You don't eat lunch in Marshport. I'll come to you."

They met at the Gray Gull. The weather was pleasant, so they sat outside on the little balcony over the water.

"Want a drink?" Jesse said when they were seated.

"No, if I do I'll have to go take a nap, and I haven't got time."

Jesse nodded.

"You have one if you want," Nina said.

"No," Jesse said. "I haven't got time, either."

They ordered iced tea. Nina looked out over the harbor. Across the water, the Paradise Yacht Club was visible.

"Long way from Marshport," she said.

"Pretty far from L.A., too," Jesse said.

"That where you're from?"

"It's where I worked before I came here," Jesse said.

"Cop?"

"Yes."

"Why'd you leave?" Nina said.

"They fired me for drinking."

"Ah," Nina said. "Another good reason not to drink at lunch."

Jesse nodded.

"What do you know about Latino gangs in Marshport," Jesse said.

"A lot. It's part of my job."

"What exactly is your job?" Jesse said.

"Do-gooder," she said. "Like you."

"I just do this for the perks," Jesse said.

"Perks?"

"Yeah, I can park where I want and I get to carry a gun."

Nina smiled.

"That's why you rode the bus with the kids and walked them into school," she said.

"Did you see my gun?" Jesse said.

Nina laughed this time.

"Okay, what do you want to know about the gangs?" she said.

"Just one," Jesse said. "Horn Street."

"Oh, my," Nina said. "The Horn Street Boys. That's Esteban Carty."

"Tell me about them."

"Twelve, fifteen kids, hang out in an abandoned garage down at the end of Horn Street. Actually, small world, one of them has a little brother at the Crowne estate project. Esteban is the, I don't know what to call him exactly, the driving force in the gang, I guess. His enforcer is a man name Puerco. Pig or Hog in English, and the name tells you mostly what you need to know. He is a fearsome psychopath. Even the cops are afraid of Puerco."

Jesse smiled.

"What?" Nina said.

"They don't have to be scared of him anymore," Jesse said.

"Something happened to Puerco?"

"He got killed a few days ago," Jesse said.

"Puerco?"

"Yep."

"God," Nina said, "I'd like to see the man who could kill Puerco."

"Anybody can kill anybody," Jesse said. "It's just a matter of what you're willing to do."

"You ever kill anyone?" Nina said.

"Yes."

They were quiet for a moment.

Then Nina said, "Esteban Carty has been on his own since he was little. I don't know what he had for family. Maybe none, ever. He's like a feral child grown up."

"So he's probably not bound by societal convention," Jesse said.

"Oh, God, no," Nina said. "That's what the gang is for."

"Any thoughts on what kind of boyfriend he'd make for a fourteen-year-old girl?" Jesse said.

She shook her head.

"Outside my purview," she said. "I'm neither a shrink nor a fourteen-year-old girl."

"But you're female and you know something about Esteban," Jesse said. "Puts you two up on me."

"I believe that one of the rules of the Horn Street Boys is that girlfriends have sex with everyone in the gang," Nina said. "All for one and one for all."

"Great for building camaraderie," Jesse said.

28.

They were naked together on the bare mattress of a rusted daybed against the wall opposite the big-screen TV in the garage at the foot of Horn Street.

"Esteban," Amber said, "what if somebody comes in?"

"Who's gonna come in 'cept Horn Street Boys?" Esteban said.

"But they'll see us."

"Won't be seeing nothing they ain't seen," Esteban said.

"I know," she said. "I'm just kind of not used to doing it like this, you know, like out in the open?"

"You moved in here. You're one of us now," Esteban said, and pressed on.

When it was over, she said, "I bet you've done a lot of girls on this couch."

"A lot," Esteban said.

"Anyone as hot as me?" she said.

"No, no, baby, you're the hottest."

There was no sound of Spanish in his voice. She wished there were. It would be more romantic. She wasn't sure he even spoke Spanish beyond a few phrases.

"So who's this dude, shot Puerco?" Esteban said.

"Wilson Cromartie," she said. "He calls himself Crow and he says he's an Apache Indian."

"I don't give a fuck he's a martian, you know? What's he want with you?"

"My daddy hired him to bring me home."

"Your daddy?"

"Yes," Amber said. "Daddy hired this guy to find me and my old lady, and kill the old lady, and bring me home."

"What's your daddy's name?"

"Louis Francisco," Amber said.

"That your real name?" Esteban said.

"Yes. Amber. Is that a sappy name? Amber Francisco."

"Yeah. Where's Daddy live?"

"Miami," Amber said. "He's very rich."

Esteban nodded.

"What's he do?"

"I don't know. He's in a bunch of businesses."

"You like him?" Esteban said.

"Hell, no," Amber said. "He's in on all kinds of shady shit, you know? And he sends me to the fucking convent school. You know? Nuns. Jesus!"

Esteban nodded.

"And he wants your old lady killed?"

"Yeah."

A couple of Horn Street Boys came into the garage. Amber rolled over onto her stomach. Neither of them paid any attention to her. They got beer from the refrigerator, sat down on a couple of rickety lawn chairs, picked up the remote from the floor, and turned on a soap opera. Amber hated soap operas. Her mother used to watch them in the big, empty house and drink beer until she fell asleep on the couch. Amber wished they'd shut it off. She wished she had her clothes on. She wished things were different.

"I think I should talk to your old man," Esteban said.

29.

Crow was sitting under the small pavilion at Paradise Beach, talking on his cell phone. The day was eighty-five and clear. The tide was in. The ocean covered most of the beach, and the waves rolled in quietly, without animosity.

"I'm not going to kill your wife, Louis," Crow said. "And I'm not going to bring your daughter down to Miami."

"You sonovabitch, Crow," Louis Francisco said at the other end of the connection. "I paid you a lot of money."

"To find them," Crow said. "I found them."

"You want to survive this, Crow, you do what I told you."

"Nope."

"If I have to come up there, by God..."

"Probably ought to," Crow said.

"Then I will," Louis Francisco said. "And I won't be coming alone."

The outrage was gone from his voice, Crow noticed. He seemed calm now. He was doing business he understood.

"I'll be here," Crow said, and turned off the cell phone.

He sat for a time looking at the ocean. He liked the ocean. There were young women on the narrow beach, in small bathing suits. He liked them, too. He stood and walked along the top of the beach and onto the causeway that led to Paradise Neck. He stopped halfway across, leaning on the wall, looking at the ocean, breathing in the clean smell of it. It would take Francisco a couple days to organize his invasion. He wondered what the cop would do with that. Stone was a cop, and this was a small town. But Stone wasn't a small-town cop. It interested Crow, how far Jesse would go. Crow was pretty sure Jesse would stick when it came down to it, that Crow could count on him. And he knew that Jesse's cops were loyal to him. The big kid, Suitcase, looked like he could handle himself. And Crow loved the feisty little female cop.

He turned and rested his back against the seawall and looked in at Paradise Harbor. Might be time to call on Marcy Campbell, too. She was good-looking, and, he was pretty sure, she was ready. He smiled. Women forgave him a lot. He watched the harbormaster's boat moving about among the tall pleasure boats riding their mooring, sails stowed, people having lunch on the afterdeck. He looked at his watch. Maybe he should have lunch. Daisy

Dyke's? No, that would be iced tea. At the Gray Gull, he could have a couple of drinks with his lunch and then go home and take a nap. He straightened and flexed his shoulders a little to loosen them, and began to walk back to the beach where his car was parked. He felt really good.

Maybe he was going to have his war.

30.

They were all there in the garage. Twelve Horn Street Boys, plus Esteban Carty. Amber sat on the floor in the corner with her arms wrapped around her knees. Listening while Esteban spoke.

"Okay," he said to the Boys, "we got a contract."

The boys seemed pleased.

"Guy gonna give us ten grand to off a broad in Paradise."

The boys responded.

"Ten grand?"

"A broad?"

"Muthafuck, man, how easy is that?"

"Easy," Esteban said.

One of the boys said something in Spanish.

"Knock it off," Esteban said. "We speak English."

Amber wondered randomly if that was some sort of self-improvement rule, or was it because Esteban didn't speak much Spanish. She shrugged mentally. The Horn Street Boys had a lot of rules.

"And here's a gas," Esteban said. "Guy paying us is Alice's father."

Everyone looked at Amber. She giggled. It was nice that Esteban told them.

"Who's the broad?" one of the boys said.

"Are you ready for this?" Esteban said.

Amber could see he was excited. She felt excited, too. He pointed at her like a referee calling a foul.

"Alice's momma," he said.

Everyone looked at her again. Amber giggled again. One of the boys started clapping, and the others joined in. Amber giggled some more, and hid her face.

"Bye-bye, Momma," Esteban said.

And the boys took up the chant.

"Bye-bye, Momma! Bye-bye, Momma! Bye-bye, Momma."

They clapped in rhythm to it and Amber, sitting on the floor, with her face in her hands and her knees up, began to rock back and forth to the chant. After a while she joined in.

"Bye-bye, Momma! Bye-bye, Momma! Bye-bye, Momma!"

"I have things to redeem," Jesse said. "But I guess so does she."

Dix inclined his head.

"She has yet to succeed at a job," Jesse said.

"Or a relationship," Dix said.

"Or a relationship," Jesse said. "We both got an oh-for on relationships."

"Except with each other," Dix said.

"This is a good relationship?" Jesse said.

"It's an enduring one," Dix said.

Jesse stared at him.

"Well," Jesse said. "Yeah, I guess so."

"Why do you think that is?"

Jesse paused.

"Love?" he said.

Dix nodded.

"And why do you think it doesn't work better?" Dix said.

"Because I'm a mess," Jesse said.

Dix shook his head almost imperceptibly.

"I'm not a mess?" Jesse said.

"*Mess* is not a very useful term in my line of work," Dix said. "But it is not unusual for someone in your circumstances to take on all the blame for those circumstances, not out of guilt but because it gives them the power to change it."

"So if it's her fault, there's nothing I can do about it," Jesse said. "And if it's my fault, there is?"

"Again, *fault* is not a term I like to use," Dix said. "But just suppose the near-fatal flaw in your relationship resides with her."

31.

"So," Jesse said. "Where were we?"

"I think you know," Dix said.

"We were wondering aloud...no, I was wondering aloud... what Jenn's career meant to her."

Dix nodded.

"I think my last question was, Do you think her career means redemption to her?"

"That's how I remember it," Dix said.

"And you were about to not answer the question," Jesse said.

Dix smiled.

"I hoped you might have a thought," he said.

"It dilutes your power a little," Dix said. "It must be very difficult to be with someone so powerful unless you yourself have power."

Jesse felt a small click in the center of himself.

"So she has to either increase her own power or decrease mine," Jesse said.

Dix pointed a forefinger at Jesse and dropped his thumb as if pretending to shoot him.

"Bingo!" Dix said.

"She's too career-driven," Jesse said.

"I would guess," Dix said, "that her ambition is a symptom, not a condition."

"A symptom of what?" Jesse said.

"She said to you something to the effect that success might be her way back to you."

"Yes," Jesse said.

He felt tense. They were about to see around a corner. He didn't know what he'd see yet, but he'd worked with Dix long enough to know that Dix, however obliquely, would bring him to it.

"But wasn't she with you before she began her career?" Dix said.

"Yes."

"So..."

Dix waited. Jesse sat. After a bit he shook his head.

"Nothing," Jesse said.

Dix whistled silently to himself, as if he were mulling something.

Then he said, "Jesse, you must know you fill a room."

Dix rarely used his first name. Jesse was pleased.

"I'm not that big," he said.

"I'm not talking about physical size," Dix said. "You are a very powerful person."

"For a drunk," Jesse said.

"The alcohol may be a saving grace," Dix said.

"Because?"